Lyle Finds His Mother

by BERNARD WABER

Houghton Mifflin Company Boston

to my godson
Joshua

Library of Congress Cataloging in Publication Data

Waber, Bernard.
  Lyle finds his mother.

  SUMMARY: Lyle the Crocodile leaves his happy home
on East 88th Street with the Primms to go in search of
his mother at the urging of his former employer Hector
P. Valenti, star of stage and screen.
  (1. Crocodiles--Fiction) I. Title.
PZ7.W113Lx   (E)   74-5336

ISBN: 0-395-19489-X REINFORCED EDITION
ISBN: 0-395-27398-6 SANDPIPER PAPERBOUND EDITION
PRINTED IN THE U.S.A.
RNF HOR PA B&B 12 11 10

The world was changing.
But if changes were taking place,
Lyle the Crocodile scarcely noticed.
It was still the same wonderful
world he loved.

Lyle's world
was Bird . . .

and Loretta, his
favorite neighbor.

It was children,
playing with children
until dark.

Most of all, Lyle's world was the house on
East 88th Street, with happy days and nights spent
close to the family he loved, the Primms.

But if Lyle was happy with his world, there was someone living across town who did not share his pleasure.

That someone was Hector P. Valenti,
Star of Stage and Screen.
Sadly, Signor Valenti had fallen
upon dark and hungry days.
His cupboard was bare. There was
not a crumb in sight.
Even the mice, who for so long
had shared his humble life, packed
up and moved one morning.

Because he could not
bear the sight of its emptiness,
Hector stored his hat in the
refrigerator; his hat and
a lonely jar of mustard.

One day, he was so overcome with hunger,
Hector began to imagine how delicious, indeed,
his hat might taste, cooked to tenderness
and seasoned lightly with mustard.

To keep his mind off his troubles,
Hector took to the streets;
only to be reminded again and again
of his empty stomach.

Even the pigeons
in the park were enjoying
excellent food, magnificent health
and outrageous cheer.
"Oh, to be a pigeon," sighed
Hector, "and never know
a day of want."

It was in the park that Hector came upon Lyle and
the Primms. The sight of Lyle brought instant memories
of happy days gone by; days when they were a team,
performing on stages the world over. He wanted to rush
up to Lyle, throw his arms around his old friend, but
shame for his ragged appearance held him back.

Lyle was everywhere in the park that day,
riding round and round on the carousel . . .

dancing about with a
huge red balloon . . .

and sailing a toy boat
with Joshua.

Wherever Lyle went,
Hector followed at a safe distance,
enjoying every minute.

When at last the Primms decided it was
time to leave the park, Lyle waved
good-bye to everyone.
"If only I could perform on stage with Lyle again,"
thought Hector, "my days of need would be
gone forever." But what reason could possibly
make Lyle ever want to leave the Primms?

On his way home, Hector came upon a sign.
It read: REMEMBER MOTHER ON MOTHER'S DAY.
In a wink, he thought of a scheme to lure
Lyle away from the Primms.
"But I can't do it," thought Hector, "not
to Lyle. No, I would rather starve."
Suddenly, a fresh and ferocious wave of
hunger swept over him.
"I'll do it," he decided.

The next day, a letter for Lyle arrived at the
house on East 88th Street.
"Dear Lyle," read Mrs. Primm. "How would you like
to meet your dear, sweet mother? If this small
matter is of interest to you, come immediately
to the address listed on the back of this letter."
And it was signed, "Cordially, Hector P. Valenti,
Star of Stage and Screen.
P.S." Hector added, "Come alone.
P.P.S. Bring along a snack."

"Come immediately indeed!" snapped Mrs. Primm.
"Hector is up to tricks again. And what a wretched trick!"
"I don't want Lyle to leave," cried Joshua.
"Lyle will stay right here where he belongs," said
Mr. Primm, "and we'll not give this letter another thought."

But Lyle gave it thought.
He gave it lots of thought.
In fact, he was astounded he had
never thought about it before.
"I didn't know I had a mother,"
he whispered to himself. "But I must
have had a mother. I'm here, aren't I?
That proves I had a mother."

It wasn't long before Lyle found
himself trying to picture his mother.
She was sort of small, he decided.
And she was very kind, like Mrs. Primm.
And she was pretty, too, like Mrs. Primm.
In fact, the more he pictured her,
the more remarkably his mother
looked like Mrs. Primm.

He began to imagine the sound
of his mother's voice.
It was sweet like Mrs. Primm's.
He was little Lyle again, and his
mother would always be saying
things like:
"Are you hungry, Lyle?
Here, have a graham cracker, dear.
Have two, as a matter of fact,
they are so delicious."

But she would be strict—his mother.
"Do wear a hat," she'd say. "And be sure
to bundle up . . . and don't dawdle . . . and be
careful crossing streets . . . and remember
not to talk to strangers . . . and behave
in school, now. Hear, Lyle?"

"My! Aren't you clever!" she would
exclaim as Lyle somersaulted, did handwalks
and showed off all of his tricks
for his mother.

It wasn't long before Lyle was deep into longing for his mother.

The Primms guessed what was going through Lyle's
mind, and they tried desperately to distract him.
Mrs. Primm, who was very active in politics,
took Lyle along with her to campaign headquarters,
where he was kept busy folding and stuffing
letters into envelopes.

Mr. Primm introduced Lyle to the
pleasures of indoor gardening.

Joshua received permission from his teacher
to bring Lyle for a visit to school.
"This is Lyle. He lives at our house. He is my
best friend," Joshua announced to the class.
"He is our friend too!" many of the
children called out.

The teacher assigned Lyle
a seat up front where everyone
could see him.
"Now, let's all show Lyle
what we are learning in school
today," he said.

Later that morning,
Lyle was given paper and
colored pencils.
This is his drawing.

At lunch, everyone wanted to sit near Lyle.
Teachers came over to introduce themselves.
"Oh, Lyle," said one teacher, "I have heard so
much about you, and I am delighted to meet you at
last. Won't you please come visit my class too?"
Lyle shook his head eagerly, and was so happy
to be asked back again.

Although he was just a bit sleepy
during math, Lyle had a marvelous
visit at school. It seemed, finally,
he had managed to forget all about
Hector — and his letter.

But he was reminded again,
several days later, when he
happened to see a mother
lovingly hand her child
a graham cracker.

And now,
not even Loretta
could coax a
smile from Lyle.

Nor could Bird.
Nor could the Primms, though they tried desperately.
In the end, and with deep sorrow in their hearts,
they made the difficult decision. They gave Lyle
their blessings to go off in search of his mother.

On the morning he was to leave,
the Primms packed a gift-basket for
Lyle to take to his mother; if in
fact, he did find her.

They packed Turkish caviar, alfalfa
dumplings, dandelion greens, yogurt
biscuits, rose petal jelly, brandied
peaches and after-dinner mints.

As a special gift, Mrs. Primm enclosed
a locket containing Lyle's picture.

The Primms then
took Lyle to Hector's
address, where they cried
their farewells.

Alone now, Lyle climbed
the six flights of stairs
to Hector's world.

"Lyle! How happy I am to see
you!" Hector greeted him.
"And you brought a gift!"

Lyle was hardly through the doorway when Hector
swooped down upon the gift-basket and began to
devour its contents.
"This is delicious!" he exclaimed between mouthfuls
of dumplings. "I must borrow the recipe."

Lyle showed Hector the letter about his mother.
"Ah, yes," sighed Hector, "but it's such a distance, you
know, to your mother. Traveling will be costly, I fear.
However, I have a wonderful plan. We can earn our way
by performing together again — if you know what I mean."
Lyle knew exactly what Hector meant.

Once again Lyle was on stage with Hector.
And magically, once again the sound of
applause rang joyously in Hector's ears.

Now, Hector was dressing expensively . . .

eating handsomely . . .

. . . and counting his money lovingly.
Every night Hector
counted his money.
And every night Lyle
showed him the letter.
"Oh that again," Hector would say,
paying it scant attention.

One night, Lyle refused to go on stage.
Hector pleaded. The stagehands shoved.
And the theater manager cried.
"Very well," said Hector,
"I will take you to your mother.
But you must perform tonight."
Lyle smiled as he moved out
onto the stage.

At last, they began the long journey
to find Lyle's mother.
They traveled for days . . .

by plane . . .

by train . . .

and by boat . . .

. . . until they reached the land of the crocodile.
Lyle looked and looked. There wasn't a crocodile
in sight; not even a ripple on the water.
"How do you like that?" said Hector. "All the way
from East 88th Street and she's not home. Well,
perhaps she's out for the day. You know how it is, Lyle.
She probably keeps herself busy. No doubt, she has
things to do and places to go. We'll just come back
another time. Maybe we'll telephone first. How's that?"
Lyle stared at him.
"I don't suppose we can telephone, can we?" said Hector.

"All right," said Hector, "if it will make you happy,
I'll call out to her."
"LYLE'S MOTHER! LYLE'S MOTHER!" Hector's singsong voice
rang out across the water. "YOU HAVE A VISITOR!
YOUR SON, LYLE, IS HERE, MOTHER, DEAR!"
Suddenly, to their astonishment, the surface of the water
broke and the head of a crocodile appeared . . .
and disappeared.

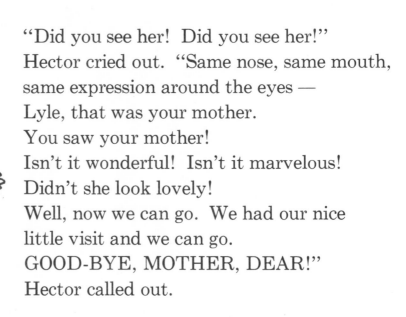

"Did you see her! Did you see her!"
Hector cried out. "Same nose, same mouth,
same expression around the eyes —
Lyle, that was your mother.
You saw your mother!
Isn't it wonderful! Isn't it marvelous!
Didn't she look lovely!
Well, now we can go. We had our nice
little visit and we can go.
GOOD-BYE, MOTHER, DEAR!"
Hector called out.

Lyle looked at him with growing suspicion.
"Well, she could have been your mother,"
said Hector. "Who is to say she wasn't your
mother? Prove it, that she wasn't your mother.
She just didn't recognize you.
You can't blame her for that. Can you?
I mean . . . well . . . what did you expect from
a stupid crocodile?" he blurted out.

Hector wanted to take back his words immediately.
"Lyle, I am sorry. I am really and truly sorry. It slipped
what I said about crocodiles. I mean . . . I think highly
of crocodiles. I adore crocodiles. Crocodiles are among my
dearest friends. Oh, Lyle, I wouldn't ever want to say anything to
hurt you. Not me. Not Hector. I would pull out my tongue first."

But before Hector
had a chance
to pull out his tongue,
the water began
to churn, and the head
of a crocodile
popped up once more.

Lyle raced toward the river.
"Don't! You mustn't! It's dangerous!" Hector
cried out as Lyle plunged into the water.
Hector shut his eyes. He opened them slowly.
To his surprise, both crocodiles were at the opposite
side of the river. And what is more, they appeared
genuinely delighted to see each other.

After a while, the two went swimming together.
They spent the entire afternoon together swimming, diving
and splashing about.
Hector grew so tired waiting for Lyle to return,
he fell asleep.

When he awakened, Lyle was standing over him.
"Is she?" said Hector. "Is she really your mother?"
Lyle motioned toward the water. Out came the other
crocodile, smiling gloriously as she suddenly began to
perform all manner of fancy somersaults, handsprings,
twirls and leaps.
Hector looked on in amazement.
"That's your mother all right," said Hector.

Several days later, the doorbell rang
at the house on East 88th Street.
Surprise! Surprise!
There stood Lyle, Hector and a very
special guest: Lyle's mother.
Bird squawked. Loretta rushed in excitedly.
And everyone shouted for joy.
"Oh, Lyle," cried Mrs. Primm, "we missed
you so much. And you found your mother!
Hello, mother!" said Mrs. Primm.

That night, they had a dinner party to
celebrate. Lyle's mother wore her lovely
locket and proudly showed Lyle's picture
to everyone.

"If ever you should be seeking
a career on stage," Hector whispered
to her, "well . . . ahem . . . perhaps
I can be helpful."

As for Lyle, his world was complete now.
He was back with the Primms, and he
had found his mother.
She wasn't quite as he had pictured her,
but then . . . a mother is still a mother.